The Rescue Princesses
The Amber Necklace

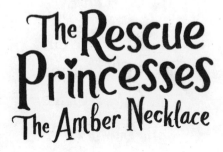

Zina crept closer to the baby lemur. She didn't want to leave him behind while she searched for his family. Would he trust her enough to let her carry him? She held out another guava, saying softly, "Are you still hungry?"

Have you read?

The Secret Promise

The Wishing Pearl

The Moonlit Mystery

The Stolen Crystals

The Snow Jewel

The Magic Rings

The Lost Gold

The Shimmering Stone

The Silver Locket

The Ice Diamond

The Rainbow Opal

The Golden Shell

The Enchanted Ruby

The Star Bracelet

The Rescue Princesses
The Amber Necklace

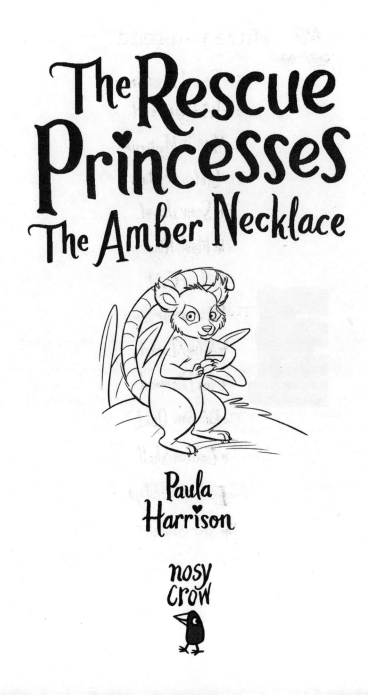

Paula
Harrison

nosy
crow

First published in the UK in 2019 by Nosy Crow Ltd
The Crow's Nest, 14 Baden Place,
Crosby Row, London SE1 1YW

Nosy Crow and associated logos are trademarks and/or registered
trademarks of Nosy Crow Ltd

Text © Paula Harrison, 2019
Cover illustration © Sharon Tancredi, 2019
Interior illustrations © Artful Doodlers, 2019

1 3 5 7 9 10 8 6 4 2

A CIP catalogue record for this book is available from the British Library

Printed and bound in Great Britain by Clays Ltd, Elcograf S.p.A.

Papers used by Nosy Crow are made from wood grown in
sustainable forests.

ISBN: 978 0 85763 989 9

www.nosycrow.com

For Hannah and Ava Carp, who enjoy
many Rescue Princess adventures
of their own

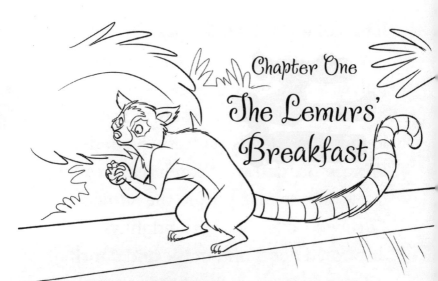

Zina crept out of the palace, shutting the door behind her. She crossed the garden, carefully holding a plate of fruit. Her bright-yellow dress swirled around her legs and an amber jewel on a silver chain hung around her neck.

The pale, glistening turrets of Ramova Palace stretched into the sapphire sky. Beyond the palace gate, tall rainforest trees swayed gently in the wind. Warm sunlight drifted through the leaves and

1

birds called in the treetops.

It was early, and no one else in the palace would be awake yet, but Zina had been too excited to stay in bed any longer. Her friends Princess Lily and Princess Scarlett were coming to stay for a few days to take part in the Ramova Carnival – a festival with brightly-decorated floats and music and dancing.

Zina was excited about the carnival but she had another secret reason for wanting to see her friends so much. They had met a few months ago at Scarlett's castle and together they had become Rescue Princesses.

This meant they'd promised always to help animals in trouble. They had already saved two baby animals! The first time, they had crossed a deep river to help a baby otter called Sparky. The next time, they'd saved an adorable little kangaroo and helped raise money for a kangaroo sanctuary. They'd even learned ninja moves so they could outsmart baddies and keep their rescues secret.

Zina climbed the steps that led to the top of the palace wall and set down the plate. She knew it would be a busy day so she wanted to make sure her most important task was done right away. Carefully, she spread the fruit along the top of the wall. Then she stood back and waited, tucking her long dark hair behind her ears.

The leaves shivered in the wind and the amber jewel on her necklace seemed to whisper back. Zina picked up the teardrop-shaped jewel and looked at it more closely. Amber from the Kingdom of Ramova was dark golden with little yellow flecks. The necklace had been given to Zina by her grandma, who had died four years ago. Her grandma had told her that amber came from tree sap and took millions of years to turn into a jewel. *It holds the heart of the forest*, she'd told Zina. *Don't ever forget that.*

A chattering noise made Zina look up. A ring-tailed lemur scampered down a tree branch and jumped on to the wall. The creature gazed at Zina with bright yellow-brown eyes, its tufted white ears pricked up and its black nose twitching.

Zina loved lemurs. They were so playful and the ring-tailed ones had beautiful furry black-and-white-striped tails. "It's all right." She smiled at the animal. "I brought the fruit for all of you. Go ahead and eat!"

The lemur galloped along the wall and picked up a piece of orange. Suddenly more lemurs swung down from the branches and jumped over to the palace wall. Last to climb down was a mother

with a little baby on her back. The lemurs
ate the banana, orange and mango
pieces, chattering noisily to each other.

"Zina! Where are you?" called Queen
Tali.

"I'm here!" Zina waved to her mum,
who was standing at the palace entrance.
Picking up the plate, she hurried down
the steps and ran back across the garden.
"I was just feeding the lemurs," she said
breathlessly.

Queen Tali smoothed her long dark
hair. She was wearing her finest dress,
made from gold silk and tied with a
green sash. "You haven't forgotten that
we have guests arriving today, have you?"

"No, I can't wait to see Lily and
Scarlett," Zina told her mum.

Queen Tali smiled. "Good! They'll all be
here by lunchtime. Could you cut some
flowers from the garden and put them

into vases? We want the palace to look its best for our visitors."

Zina beamed. "I'd love to! I'll get started straightaway."

Zina felt excitement rising like a balloon inside her all morning. She began to feel a little shy too – she hadn't seen her friends for weeks and weeks. What if they didn't like the Kingdom of Ramova or the palace very much? She frowned at her reflection in her bedroom mirror as she brushed her long dark hair and tied it up with a ribbon. She had to be braver, she told herself, and remember what good friends Lily and Scarlett were.

She glanced at the diamond ring that she wore every day. The Rescue Princesses often used magic jewels when they needed to help animals in trouble. They all had special rings that let them talk to

7

each other when they were apart. To use the ring, all Zina had to do was press the heart-shaped jewel. For a moment, she wanted to touch the diamond, watch it light up and talk to her friends. Then she reminded herself they would be here very soon!

Hurrying out into the garden, she cut some rosy periwinkle flowers and some bright-red zinnias. She checked the top of the palace wall and was delighted to see all the lemurs' fruit was gone. Gathering up the flowers, she went inside to look for the royal vases.

Just before lunch, a black and gold carriage rolled through the gates. It drew to a stop in front of the palace steps and Scarlett burst out, her curly black hair bouncing. She ran to Zina, who'd been waiting by the front door, and hugged her. "Thanks for inviting us!" she said, beaming. "Are you ready for some more Rescue Princess adventures?"

"Shh, Scarlett! Someone will hear you," said Lily. "Hi, Zina!" She came up the steps, her blonde hair falling over her shoulders.

Zina smiled shyly. "Hi, Lily. Hi, Scarlett."

Queen Tali came hurrying out of the palace door. "Welcome to the Kingdom of Ramova. How was your journey, girls?"

"It was great!" Scarlett's eyes sparkled. "I kept looking out of the window at the clouds and thinking that they looked like fluffy bunny tails or sheep or scrunched-up pillows ... and when we went through the forest the carriage got really bumpy and I thought it was like driving a tractor round a track for racing cars. Not that I've actually done that!"

Queen Tali looked stunned for a moment and Zina couldn't help grinning.

She'd forgotten how chatty Scarlett could be! "Well, I'm glad you enjoyed the carriage ride," the queen said at last. "I must say hello to your parents." She went to greet the kings and queens as they climbed out of the carriage.

Looking at her friends, Zina felt her shyness melting away. "There's so much I want to show you." She linked arms with Lily and Scarlett. "We're going to have the best time ever!"

Chapter Two
The Carnival Master

Queen Tali bustled up the steps. "Shall we go inside, everyone? I'm sure you'd all like a drink and a slice of cake after your long journey." She glanced at the palace gate. "Oh, this is a surprise! I wasn't expecting the Carnival Master till tomorrow."

A bright-yellow wagon drew up behind the carriage and a man climbed down from the driver's seat. He was wearing a purple jacket, trousers made from multicoloured patches and a tall black hat. "Good morning, Your Majesties." He took off his hat and swept a deep bow.

"Everyone – this is Mr Hazzam, who organises our carnival every year," said Queen Tali. "Come inside and tell us how you're getting on, Mr Hazzam." She led them all into the parlour and rang the bell for refreshments.

Zina's dad, King Tomas, came in and shook everyone's hand. Then he began explaining to the other kings and queens all the detailed plans for the carnival. Mr Hazzam joined in, describing the banners and garlands that would be hanging along the parade route.

"I've really been looking forward to the carnival," Lily said quietly to Zina as they sat down. "Will there be lots of music?"

"Yes, music and dancing, and the costumes are amazing!" Zina told her.

"My favourite part is the floats. They're carts decorated with all kinds of things and they roll past the crowds one after the other."

Mr Hazzam overheard her and smiled. "I believe you'll be pleased with our floats this year, Princess Zina. The animal ones are especially good! The parrot float is brightly coloured and the ocean float has pretend jellyfish and lots of seashells. The only disappointment is the lemur float, which isn't finished because the person in charge broke their ankle. I think we're going to have to leave that one out this year."

"That's a shame!" Queen Tali thanked the maids, who had brought in a large cake with lemon icing, cups of tea and some glasses of cherryade.

Zina sipped her cherryade thoughtfully. It would be a shame not to have a lemur float in the parade. After all, lemurs were one of the best-known animals in Ramova. A sudden thought popped into her head. Maybe *they* could decorate the lemur float! She exchanged looks with Lily, who loved doing art and decorating things.

"Lily, do you think we should ask to decorate the float?" she whispered.

"Yes! Ask them, Zina," Lily whispered back.

Zina swallowed and tried to think of the right thing to say. What if they thought it was a silly idea?

Scarlett nudged her with an elbow and nodded.

Zina took a deep breath. "Um ... Mr Hazzam..."

The Carnival Master was busy talking to Lily's mum and took a few moments to turn round. "Did you want to ask me something, Princess Zina?"

"Well, I was just wondering... Could *we* decorate the lemur float? I love lemurs and it would be awful not to have the float in the parade." Zina's cheeks grew hot and she felt as if everyone was looking at her.

"That's a very kind offer!" exclaimed Mr Hazzam. "I'd be very grateful for the help. I could bring the float to the palace this afternoon and leave it here for you to work on." He glanced at the kings and queens.

Queen Tali was nodding but Scarlett's parents, the King and Queen of Deronda, looked doubtful. "Will it be very messy?" asked Scarlett's mum.

"I'm sure it won't." Scarlett pushed aside her black curls. "Please, mum! It sounds great fun."

At last all the kings and queens agreed

that the girls could decorate the float ready for the carnival.

"But what do lemurs look like?" cried Scarlett, once the grown-ups had left to look around the palace. "I've never even seen one. Are they like leopards?"

"I think they're more like monkeys," said Lily. "I've looked at pictures of them in my geography book at home."

"There are lots of different kinds but the ring-tailed lemurs are the most common ones in this part of the forest," said Zina. "I could show them to you if you like?"

"Yes! Let's go right now." Scarlett jumped up, nearly knocking over the plate of lemon cake.

"Seeing them will give us ideas for the float," agreed Lily.

Zina knew the lemurs wouldn't return to the palace wall till breakfast time the next morning, so she led the other princesses across the garden and through the tall palace gate. Then she took them down a little winding path among the trees.

"There's a cluster of tamarind trees not far away, where the lemurs like to play," she told the others. "The tamarind fruit is their favourite food so they're sure to be there!"

Soon the gate and the palace walls were far behind. The trees leaned close together, their roots jutting out of the dark earth. The leaves rustled and Zina thought she heard her amber jewel whispering back softly.

"This place is amazing," gasped Scarlett. "Look at that parrot."

The parrot whistled and ruffled its yellow feathers. Then a bright-green lizard darted up a nearby tree trunk, its tongue flicking.

"That's a gecko," Zina told them. "They're cute, aren't they? I don't know where the lemurs have gone. There are usually lots of them in this part of the forest."

They walked on a little further, stopping by a circle of trees with long, knobbly fruit hanging from the branches. A cluster of bright-eyed lemurs sprang down from the treetops. One of them paused to look at the girls, its beautiful black-and-white tail pointing straight up.

"If we keep still we won't scare them," Zina said quietly.

"They're lovely," whispered Scarlett, as three more lemurs jumped down. "Look at the baby!"

The mother lemur with the baby on her back reached the ground last. The creatures began looking around the forest floor for food, their tails all pointing upwards. The little baby clambered down from his mother's back and began searching among the twigs and fallen leaves.

"They're used to me because I feed them fruit for breakfast every day," Zina explained.

"I didn't think they'd be so furry." Scarlett crept a little closer and one of the lemurs scampered across her shoe, making them all giggle.

"They have lovely golden-brown eyes too," said Lily. "Have you ever touched one, Zina?"

Zina was about to reply when a roaring noise made her jump.

A rusty blue truck came crashing through the bushes, stopping just outside the clearing. The lemurs screeched in alarm and galloped away into the trees. A group of men and women wearing yellow helmets climbed out of the truck and one of them began marking the tree trunks with a thick red marker.

"Bring me the rope," called a man with a thick beard. "We'll come back and cut all these trees down tomorrow."

A cold prickle ran down Zina's neck. Cut down the trees? They couldn't do that. This place was the lemurs' home!

Chapter Three

A Rainforest Home

A man and a woman wearing yellow helmets began tying a rope around the circle of trees. Zina felt as if her voice was stuck in her throat. Why were these people here? And how had they got the truck through the forest? The trees grew so close together it should have been impossible.

Scarlett bounded forward. "Hold on a minute! This is where the lemurs live – don't you care about them?"

The people with the rope looked round in surprise. "Where did you come from?" the woman asked suspiciously. "Ando, there's some children here."

The bearded man came over. "Stand back, please. We're roping off this area so that tomorrow we can come back and cut down these trees."

"But you can't!" Zina burst out. "This part of the rainforest is the lemurs' home."

"I'm sorry, young lady, but the carnival will be passing this way. Part of the main road is flooded after all the rain last week so we're making a shortcut for the floats. We've already cleared the trees up to this point." He beckoned them to the edge of the clearing and pointed through the bushes. A line of tree stumps stretched into the distance and logs were piled up on the ground.

Zina's heart sank. How could they destroy such a long stretch of beautiful trees?

The workman looked at Zina more closely. "Have I seen you before? You look very familiar."

Zina blushed. "I'm Princess Zina from the palace and these are my friends, Princesses Scarlett and Lily."

"I beg your pardon, Princess Zina. I didn't recognise you at first. My name's Ando." The bearded man smiled and did a clumsy bow. "We really do need to clear these trees so that the carnival can get through. There's too much water on the road."

"But the lemurs live here," said Zina. "These tamarind trees give them leaves and fruit to eat when the other trees are bare. And these are the only tamarind trees I've seen in the whole forest!"

"If this place is so important why aren't the lemurs here now?" said the woman, tying the rope around the last tree.

Zina swallowed. "They *were* here just now but they ran away when your truck came along." But the woman had turned away to gather up the spare rope and didn't even answer.

Ando checked each roped-off tree. Then he called everyone back to the truck, giving the girls one last wave before they rolled away through the bushes.

"The poor lemurs!" said Zina. "No other trees in the forest provide food all year round like the tamarind trees. The lemurs will starve without them."

"You should have told them that, Zina," said Scarlett.

"I tried!" Zina's face grew hot. She wished she'd explained things better to the grown-ups but they'd left and it was too late. "I've been looking forward to the carnival so much. I never thought the parade would end up hurting the lemurs."

Scarlett put her hands on her hips. "Those carnival people didn't even listen to us! They just drove in and tied their rope and left."

"I don't think they understood how special these trees are," said Zina sadly.

"Maybe we should go after them. Use ninja moves to follow the truck," said Scarlett.

"Wait a minute!" Lily ducked under the ring of rope and ran into the clearing. "I saw something move."

The others scrambled after her. "What did it look like?" asked Zina. "Was it an insect?"

"I think it's a lot bigger than that." Lily pointed to a bump sticking out of a nearby pile of leaves. The leaves quivered and a little furry head with tufted ears popped up.

"It's the baby lemur!" cried Scarlett. "Why is he here by himself?"

"He must have been left behind," said Zina.

Lily crouched down beside the baby lemur. The little creature shrank away from her and his stripy tail drooped. "Don't be scared. We won't hurt you." She reached out to touch him but the lemur dashed away and hid behind the nearest tree trunk.

"He might be hungry." Zina picked up a green guava that was lying on the ground and crept towards the lemur, trying not to startle him. The creature peeked at her with big golden-brown eyes. Then at last he scampered out from behind the tree and took the guava in his paws.

"That's it!" Zina whispered gently. "You can trust us."

"Isn't he adorable?" cooed Lily.

"He's lovely," agreed Zina.

The baby lemur nibbled the fruit, his tail waving gently. Zina stroked his soft fur and velvety ears.

"Poor thing! He's too young to be away from his family." Scarlett tiptoed over to Zina's side. "But at least he has us to help him."

Lily nodded. "This is definitely a job for the Rescue Princesses! But how can we find the other lemurs? The forest seems enormous and they could be anywhere."

"I can sometimes track the lemurs if I listen hard for their movements," said Zina. "You're right, Scarlett. A lemur this young shouldn't be alone in the forest. We have to help him find his family again."

Chapter Four

The Lemur that was Left Behind

Zina crept closer to the baby lemur. She didn't want to leave him behind while she searched for his family. Would he trust her enough to let her carry him? She held out another guava, saying softly, "Are you still hungry?"

The little lemur tilted his head and darted forward a few steps.

"I think he's starting to get used to us," whispered Lily.

Slowly, Zina moved the fruit to her

left shoulder. Then she stayed very still, holding her breath. The baby lemur crept forward a little more, his tail swaying. Then at last he jumped on to Zina's knee and scampered up her arm. Stopping at her shoulder, he began nibbling the delicious green fruit.

"He likes you!" cried Lily. "Can I stroke him?"

"It's better if you don't just yet," said Zina quickly. "He's quite shy and I don't want him to run away."

Scarlett marched across the clearing and ducked under the rope. "I think the lemurs went this way."

Lily ran after Scarlett, but Zina followed more slowly. She didn't want to scare the baby lemur by starting to run. He clung to her shoulder, still nibbling the fruit.

Zina murmured soothingly to him,

"Don't worry. We'll look after you."

The princesses pushed their way through the undergrowth and leapt across a stream full of croaking frogs. Long vines hung snake-like from the trees and lizards dived into the bushes as they passed. The leaves on the topmost branches of the trees fluttered like a thousand tiny flags.

Zina put a hand to her amber necklace. This was deeper inside the rainforest than she'd ever gone before. With every step she took, the amber jewel seemed to whisper a little louder. She caught her breath. What did the whispering mean?

She stopped for a moment and lifted the silver necklace, letting the jewel spin gently. Sunlight breaking through the leaves caught the golden stone and lit up tiny yellow flecks at its centre.

The lemur chattered softly into her ear, bringing Zina out of her daydream. Scarlett and Lily had gone on ahead.

"Wait!" she called, hurrying to catch up with them. "We don't want to get lost. Let's mark the trees so we can find our way back." She picked up a castina flower and made a brightly coloured dot on the tree using the flower's orange pollen.

Scarlett pushed her dark curls away from her face. "I thought we would have found the lemurs by now but it's so hard to see through these trees."

"The best way to find something in the rainforest is to listen," Zina told them. "We can't see very far but we'll still hear the lemurs if they're close by."

The princesses stood still and listened very hard.

Lily frowned. "All I can hear is those

frogs by the stream. I didn't realise such small creatures could be so loud!"

"We should split up and go in different directions," Scarlett decided. "That way we have more chance of finding the lemurs."

"No, we mustn't!" Zina's face was serious. "It's really easy to get lost if you don't know the forest. Then you could be trying to find your way back for hours! Let's go a little further and see if we can spot signs of where the lemurs have been."

The princesses walked on, straining for the sound of creatures scampering through the trees.

Zina paused beside a fallen log. "See that fruit peel?" She pointed to the ground. "That looks like it was dropped here today. We could be close!"

"Isn't there a quicker way to find them?

How about I climb this tree?" Scarlett's eyes sparkled as she swung herself up into the branches.

"OK, I'll wait here." Zina stroked the baby lemur's head.

"I'll stay too," Lily said quickly. "The branches might not be strong enough for two people at once."

Scarlett clambered on until she disappeared into a mass of leaves and only her feet were visible. "I can see loads from up here. I can see the top of the palace *and* I can see the part of the road that's flooded."

"What about the lemurs?" called Lily.

"There are some branches swaying to the left, but I don't know if it's just the wind moving them." Scarlett climbed down before leaping to the ground.

Zina pushed aside some fallen leaves

with her toe. "There's more fruit peel just here. That's two clues that point us this way!"

The princesses sped up, squeezing past bushes and clambering over knobbly tree roots. The baby lemur nestled close to Zina's ear and wrapped his tail around her neck. Then suddenly his ears pricked up and he gave a little squeak.

"Did you hear something?" Zina whispered to him.

A moment later she heard it too. Leaves rustled and there was the faint sound of lemurs calling.

Zina gathered the baby lemur in her arms and ran. She was determined to find his family before they moved on again.

As the girls raced into the clearing, the creatures squawked to each other and sprang higher into the trees.

Breathlessly, Zina set the baby lemur down on the ground and slowly backed away. Lily and Scarlett crept backwards too.

The little lemur squeaked and his mother sprang down from the trees. The baby jumped on to her back, chattering happily. The other lemurs slowly came out of hiding. They slipped down from the branches and went on searching for food on the forest floor.

"They seem different – almost like they're sad." Lily's brow wrinkled.

"They're not talking to each other as much as usual. Maybe that's why it took us so long to hear them." Zina watched the creatures worriedly. Were they unhappy about being chased away from the tamarind trees? If the trees were cut down tomorrow, it would leave the lemurs without enough food. "We have to do something!" she burst out.

"About the lemurs and their special trees, you mean?" asked Lily.

"Yes, we can't let those workmen take the trees away. The lemurs need them!" Zina's mind whirled. "Maybe we could move the rope they tied around the trees. Then, when they return, they won't know which ones to cut down any more."

"Why don't you talk to your mum and dad, Zina," suggested Scarlett. "They could order the workmen to change the route for the carnival."

Zina bit her lip. Her parents got so busy at carnival time that it was hard to get their attention. With visitors staying at the palace it would be even worse. But this was so important to the lemurs, she had to try. "I'll talk to them,"

she told Scarlett. "Come on – the palace
is this way."

Chapter Five

A Secret Plan

By the time Zina, Scarlett and Lily reached the palace, they were hot and tired, and had bits of leaves stuck to their hair. Zina left her friends drinking lemonade on the terrace and went to look for her mum and dad. At last she found them in the royal kitchen talking to the cook. "Mum ... Dad ... something awful has happened," she began.

"Just a minute, Zina." Her mum was scribbling on a pad of paper. "So that's roast lamb with fried mango, and chicken pie with tarragon. But what about dessert?"

Zina sighed and tried not to look impatient.

"Perhaps we could have star fruit pancakes with strawberry sauce," said King Tomas. "I'm sure everyone will like that."

"Hmm, perhaps." Queen Tali's forehead wrinkled. "But does it really go with the roast lamb for main course?"

"Mum, can I talk to you about something?" asked Zina.

"Yes, just a moment." The queen stared at her scribbled menu. "Thank you, Cook. I'll think about it a little longer but we should definitely have the roast lamb for the main course." The cook bobbed a curtsy and hurried away.

The queen turned to her daughter

and her smile dropped. "Zina, what happened to your hair? And what are those marks on your dress?"

Zina combed her fingers through her tangled black hair and brushed the earth off her dress. "We went into the rainforest to look at the lemurs. We thought it would give us some ideas for decorating the float."

"Did you get any good ideas?" asked her dad, smiling.

"Well, not yet." Zina noticed that her mum was still frowning, but she carried on. "And we ran into some carnival workers. They're changing the route of the carnival because of the flooded road. They plan to chop down the tamarind trees, which is an awful idea. They're the only trees that give the lemurs food all year round."

"Oh, yes." Her mum glanced back at

her menu.

"Can't you stop them?" said Zina desperately. "The lemurs love those trees and without them they'll find it hard to get enough food."

"Don't worry," her dad told her. "There's lots of fruit in the forest, especially at this time of year."

"But in a few months' time that fruit will be gone. Only the tamarind trees will still have fruit and leaves." Zina's voice rose. Her parents didn't look worried at all. Why didn't they understand? "Please! If you tell Mr Hazzam that the route is wrong we can stop the trees from being destroyed and save the lemurs."

"That's enough, Zina!" her mum cut in. "I think you're being a little silly. Just because you feed the lemurs every morning doesn't mean they're your pets. I'm sure they'll be absolutely fine."

"And you don't know for sure that those are the only tamarind trees in the forest, do you?" her dad put in.

Zina's cheeks blazed. "No, but I've never seen any others."

"I'm sorry, my darling, but we're just so busy sorting out menus for the banquets and then there's the carnival to organise." Queen Tali gave Zina a quick smile as she swept out of the kitchen. King Tomas patted her arm before following the queen out of the door.

Zina tried to swallow but there was a lump in her throat. She knew there were lots of other trees in the forest but the tamarind trees were special and the lemurs needed them. She walked slowly back to meet her friends.

Lily jumped up as she came on to the terrace. "Oh no! Is it bad news?" she asked.

Zina nodded. "My parents think there are plenty of other places for the lemurs to live. They don't understand that those trees are special."

"Then we just have to find another way to save the trees." Scarlett drank the rest of her lemonade in one gulp. "All we need is a plan!"

Just then, Queen Tali came outside with Scarlett's parents, the King and Queen of Deronda. Behind them was a maid carrying a tray of coffee cups.

Zina thought quickly. "I haven't shown you my room yet," she said to the other girls. She needed to talk to Lily and Scarlett without the grown-ups hearing!

Lily understood straightaway. "I'd love to see your room. Have you got many tiaras?"

"I've got four. Come and see." Zina led them inside. The palace corridor was made from smooth white marble, and tropical plants with huge, hand-shaped leaves were dotted all over the place.

Zina's room was at the end of the corridor. Her bed was scattered with brightly coloured cushions and she had special shelves above her dressing table piled high with tiaras and other jewellery.

"I love this one." Scarlett picked up a silver tiara dotted with diamonds.

"Thanks." Zina smiled. "But I really wanted to bring you here so we could talk about what to do. How can we stop those carnival workers from chopping down the lemurs' trees?"

They were all silent for a moment.

"Maybe there's a magic jewel that can help us," said Scarlett at last. "We could make one that scares the loggers away."

"I don't think any jewel – even a magic one – could do that," said Lily. "But

perhaps we could build a bridge over the flooded road."

Zina curled her hair behind her ear. "I think that would be tricky. The flood sounds really bad."

They were all silent again. Then an idea popped into Zina's head. "Maybe we can ask them to change the path through the forest. We just have to make them care about the lemurs. Then they'll understand how important the tamarind trees really are!"

Scarlett plonked herself down on Zina's bed. "But they wouldn't listen today so they won't be any different tomorrow."

Zina's mind was spinning. Ando, the leader, had been very polite. He just hadn't understood why the trees were important. "We have to show them the lemurs – make them see what amazing animals they are."

Lily's eyes lit up. "You could tell them lots of facts about the lemurs – how they live in groups and what they like to eat. You'd need to make sure the lemurs don't run away again."

Zina thought hard. "If we take them lots of fruit they'll definitely stay! I know what they like because I take them breakfast every morning."

Scarlett frowned a little. "It all sounds like a lot of talking. I like it better when we climb trees and wade across rivers."

"You will help, won't you, Scarlett?" asked Zina.

Scarlett grinned. "Of course I will! Rescue Princesses always have to work as a team."

Chapter Six

A Special Fruit Salad

Zina woke up the next day buzzing with excitement. She felt sure the plan to save the lemurs' special trees would work. She woke Scarlett and Lily, and they sneaked downstairs to the kitchen.

"Goodness me – three princesses!" said Cook. "You're up very early. Couldn't you wait any longer for breakfast?"

"We came to get the fruit for the lemurs," explained Zina.

Just then, Lily's stomach gave an

enormous gurgle. "But maybe we could take some breakfast with us too," she said, giggling.

Zina always chopped the lemurs' fruit herself each morning. Today she put in lots of mango and bananas because she knew the lemurs loved them. Lily helped her gather the fruit salad into a wooden bowl and they added it to the picnic basket that Cook had filled with rolls and pastries.

"I see the lemurs get extra fruit today," said Cook, smiling. "I hope they enjoy it."

"Thank you, Cook." Zina took the basket and closed the lid. But when she reached the back door, she spotted Lily's mum and Scarlett's parents walking round the garden.

"What shall we do?" she whispered to the others. "I'm not supposed to go out into the forest each morning until I've done two pages of neat handwriting and practised my curtsies a hundred times."

"But we have to go – it's an emergency!" Scarlett frowned. "We could use ninja moves and then they won't see us."

Lily's eyes lit up. "I brought ninja clothes for all of us in my suitcase – I made them with my mum's sewing machine. We could wear them right now."

"You actually made them?" Scarlett's eyes widened. "Can we try them on?"

The princesses dashed upstairs to Lily's room and changed into the dark-green tops, which were decorated with a leafy pattern, and black leggings. Then they admired the ninja clothes in the mirror.

"These are great, Lily!" cried Scarlett. "We'll be really well camouflaged against the trees."

"Thanks for making them." Zina smiled at her friend. Lily had found ninja moves quite tricky to learn when they'd first become Rescue Princesses. Zina thought it was really sweet of her to sew the ninja clothes. It would make creeping around without being seen a lot easier!

Lily grinned. "They work really well!"

"We'd better hurry." Zina picked up the basket again. "We have to get to the clearing before the carnival workers do."

The princesses crept downstairs and out of the back door. Keeping a sharp eye on the grown-ups, they slipped across the garden one by one. Zina sprinted over to a tall tree and ducked behind the trunk. Then she beckoned to Lily to follow her. Scarlett hid behind a nearby statue.

They waited for a long time while Scarlett's parents studied a yellow butterfly fluttering around the palace

wall. Then at last the grown-ups turned
away and the girls tiptoed through the
silver palace gates.

Zina glanced up at the palace wall
as they left. It was too early for the
lemurs to be here. The creatures would
be so surprised when she brought their
breakfast into the rainforest for a change!

"Shall I carry the basket?" said Lily.
"Then you can lead the way."

"Thanks!" Zina passed her basket to Lily
and looked around for the right path. She
took them through a narrow archway of
trees where bright-red and purple flowers
dotted the forest floor like jewels. A bird
with beautiful blue feathers fluttered to a
nearby tree and watched them curiously.

"What's that, Zina?" Scarlett pointed to
the bird.

"It's a blue coua. They're pretty, aren't
they?" replied Zina. "And look, there's

a panther chameleon. They can change colour to match their surroundings."

The pink-and-yellow-striped lizard swivelled one eye in their direction before running down a tree trunk and disappearing into the undergrowth.

As the princesses walked deeper into the forest, the trees grew closer and their leaves wove together like an emerald-green roof. Branches bobbed in the wind and flecks of sunlight danced across the forest floor. Zina's amber jewel whispered to the rustling leaves.

"What was that?" asked Lily curiously. "Did your necklace make a sound?"

"Look – lemurs!" interrupted Scarlett.

A troop of ring-tailed lemurs bounded through the trees. Zina's heart skipped a beat as she led the way into the clearing and set the picnic basket down on the ground. "I'm so glad we got here before

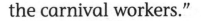

the carnival workers."

"Shall we give the lemurs their breakfast now or wait till those people come?" asked Scarlett.

A few lemurs scampered to the ground and one galloped right up to the picnic basket.

"Let's give them some now – they look hungry." Zina rummaged in the basket. "I chopped up a lot of fruit so we'll still have some left over."

The girls spread half of the fruit across the ground. Then they climbed on to a large mossy stone at the side of the clearing and shared Cook's pastries.

The lemurs nibbled the fruit hungrily. Then they began leaping around the clearing, chasing each other and swinging off the rope that the carnival workers had tied around the trees.

At last there was a rumbling sound and

a blue truck rolled through the bushes. The bearded man, Ando, climbed out and two workmen followed him. The lemurs sprang into the trees, calling in alarm.

Scarlett quickly flung the rest of the fruit on to the ground. The lemurs waited for a moment, watching the workmen warily. Then they slipped down from the trees and began to eat.

"Good luck!" Lily squeezed Zina's arm. "At least there aren't as many of them this time."

Zina brushed off the pastry crumbs and walked towards the workmen. Suddenly her hands were hot and her mouth felt dry. *You have to remember lots of lemur facts*, she told herself firmly. *Don't let them go before you've explained things properly.*

"Your Highness." Ando looked at Zina's green ninja clothes in surprise. "I really must ask you to leave this area.

We'll begin sawing soon and it'll be very dangerous."

Zina took a deep breath. "I'd like you to listen to me first. There's a lot you don't know about the lemurs that live here. Please would you come and sit down?"

Ando took off his yellow helmet and scratched his head. "I suppose so. Just for a minute." He sat on the mossy stone and his workmates joined him.

Zina felt as if everyone's eyes were fixed on her. She stared at the little baby lemur, who was nibbling a piece of mango, and tried to remember what she'd planned to say.

"Go on, Zina," whispered Lily. "You can do it."

Zina swallowed. "Ring-tailed lemurs live in groups of fifteen to twenty animals. As well as fruit, they eat flowers, leaves and sap." She noticed the workmen smiling as they watched the animals playing, and her heart lifted. "When lemurs look for food on the ground, they point their tails straight up so that everyone stays together and no one gets lost."

"I didn't know that," said Ando. "What else can you tell us, Princess Zina?"

Zina explained why the tamarind trees were so special, providing food all year round. "The lemurs are amazing animals. That's why we want to save the trees that give them food for the whole year." She clasped her hands together. "So please will you change the route of the carnival parade? Then the lemurs can keep the trees they need so much."

Ando's eyebrows rose. "I didn't realise these trees were so important. I'm glad you told us in time."

"Then you'll change the carnival route and leave the tamarind trees alone?"

Scarlett asked eagerly.

Ando looked at the lemurs bounding along the ground and scampering through the branches. "Yes, I definitely will!"

Chapter Seven

A Truck Ride Through the Forest

Zina beamed with delight as the men untied the rope around the trees. She'd done it! She'd persuaded the workmen that the lemurs should keep their home.

"We'll need to find a new path for the carnival floats." Ando took a map out of the truck and studied it closely. "Princess Zina, would you and your friends help us? You can check whether the new route crosses any more tamarind trees."

Zina exchanged looks with Scarlett

and Lily.

"We should definitely help!" whispered Scarlett, her eyes sparkling.

Zina turned to Ando. "We'd be happy to help you. We'd like to protect as much of the forest as we can."

"If you climb into the truck we'll give you a ride," said Ando. "We must go back to the start of the route by the main road."

The princesses grinned in delight and climbed into the back of Ando's truck.

"This is so much fun!" said Scarlett, holding tight to the side as the truck bumped its way through the bushes. "Just imagine what our parents would say."

Zina bit her lip. She didn't think her mum would be very impressed to see her riding in a truck wearing ninja clothes!

A few minutes later, the truck rumbled out of the forest next to the road. Ando

stopped and the girls jumped down from the back. A whole section of the road was covered with water. The river, which had flooded over the top of its banks, lay just beyond.

"This is where the path was supposed to go." Ando unfolded the map and drew a line with his finger. "We chose this route so that it joined the road on the other side. We've already cut down half the trees."

Zina studied the map. She could see the large square shape of the palace and the forest beside it. Close by was the city, where the carnival parade would begin.

"How far does the flood go?" asked Scarlett.

"The water stretches all the way to here." Ando pointed to the map again.

"So if you take the path along like

this it'll join the road a little quicker," suggested Lily. "You'll have less trees to chop down and that means you'll disturb less animals too."

Zina nodded. "Yes – make the path shorter! There are lots of creatures living in the forest, not just the ring-tailed lemurs."

"Thank you, princesses." Ando folded up the map. "Follow me and I'll show you where the new path will go." He led the princesses along the path where some trees had already been felled. Logs lay in neat piles at the side.

As the girls checked the new route for tamarind trees, the workmen walked behind them marking the new path by putting chalk crosses on the trees.

"There are no tamarind trees along the path at all," said Zina, as they rejoined the road.

"That's good news!" Ando smiled. "Thank you, princesses. I hope I'll see you again on Carnival Day."

"Goodbye!" The girls waved as they walked on down the road towards the palace.

"We did it!" Scarlett skipped through the palace gates, her black curls bobbing. "What shall we do now?"

"We could get something to eat," suggested Lily. "I'm really hungry."

A maid came down the palace steps to meet them. "Good morning, Princess Zina." Her eyes widened a little when she saw their odd green clothes. "Your parents took the other kings and queens for a tour of the City Gardens. Queen Tali wanted me to let you know that the float has arrived and it's in the courtyard ready for decorating."

"Thank you," said Zina.

The maid curtsied and went back inside.

Lily's eyes lit up. "I can't wait to make the perfect lemur float."

Zina smiled. She knew how much Lily loved making things. She was sure her friend would have lots of ideas. "The carnival is tomorrow so we'd better get started!"

They hurried through the palace garden and found the wooden carnival float standing in the courtyard.

"It looks so big and empty," said Scarlett.

"But it won't be when we've finished," said Lily excitedly. "First we need to fix paper here at the back and paint a rainforest background on it. Then we can make tall trees out of rolled-up cardboard and stick branches and leaves on to them. Do you have any cardboard, Zina?"

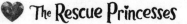

"I think so," replied Zina. "Let's collect all the things we need."

The princesses gathered cardboard, paper, glue, scissors and paint. Lily began painting the rainforest background, while Scarlett and Zina rolled up the cardboard to make the tree trunks.

They fixed the cardboard tree trunks to the cart with sticky tape and made sure none of them wobbled. Then Zina started cutting out green tissue-paper leaves.

Lily studied the float, curling her blonde hair behind her ear. "It would look nice if we added some flowers."

"We can pick a few from the garden," said Zina. "And I'll fetch the furry toy lemurs from my bedroom. We can put them in the cardboard trees."

At last they stopped to look at the decorated float. The cardboard trees stood tall and straight, and Zina's toy

lemurs peeped between the beautiful tissue-paper leaves.

Lily tilted her head to one side. "It just needs a little more decoration... Maybe we could hang some vines from the branches and scatter some twigs across the floor – just to make it look real."

Rushing through the palace gates, the princesses gathered twigs and low-hanging vines from the nearby trees.

Zina stopped suddenly. "I think I left the picnic basket behind in the forest where we met Ando and the workmen. I forgot all about it."

"We can fetch it now," said Scarlett, and the girls headed deeper into the trees.

The rainforest was eerily quiet. No parrots squawked overhead. No lizards rustled in the bushes. There was only the endless fluttering of leaves in the wind and Zina's amber jewel murmuring back.

"Zina, why does your necklace make that whispering sound?" Lily stared at it curiously.

"I don't know." Zina lifted the golden jewel on its chain. "It always happens when I'm out in the forest. Amber comes from tree sap, which turns into a jewel over millions of years. My grandma used to say it holds the heart of the forest."

"It's really beautiful," said Lily.

"Hey! We're nearly there," called Scarlett, who'd climbed halfway up a tree. "I can't hear the lemurs though."

Zina hurried forward. She was sure she recognised the way. The bushes and flowers looked just the same. Yet just up ahead there was a huge open patch of blue sky where branches and leaves should have been.

A horrible cold feeling ballooned in Zina's stomach. She darted past some

bushes and gasped. Sunlight beamed down through the empty space. Eight large tree stumps stuck out of the ground and sawdust was scattered all around the clearing.

The special tamarind trees were gone.

Chapter Eight

A Terrible Mistake

Zina's eyes filled with tears. "No! Why did they take these trees when they said they wouldn't?"

"It's horrible!" stormed Scarlett. "We told them the lemurs needed the tamarind trees. We even helped them change the carnival route."

"The lemurs are gone too," said Lily. "They must have run away when the carnival workers started sawing."

Zina sank on to one of the stubby tree

stumps. She couldn't believe this had once been a beautiful tamarind tree with long branches and emerald-green leaves. A pile of sawn-off branches stacked to one side was all that was left.

A rumbling began in the distance, growing louder. A blue truck rolled to a stop and Ando jumped out. "Princess Zina, I was just on my way to the palace to find you. I'm so sorry about these trees."

Zina wiped a tear from the corner of her eye. She couldn't think of anything to say.

Ando scratched his head anxiously. "It was all a terrible mistake! You see, some of my team didn't come with me this morning. They were busy hanging up carnival decorations and when they finished early, they drove out to find us. When they saw these trees still standing they got on with cutting them down because they thought it needed to be done."

"You mean they didn't know you were changing the route of the parade?" said Lily.

"Exactly." Ando gave a deep sigh. "I can only tell you again how sorry I am about all this." He bowed before returning to his truck.

"So it was all a mistake," said Scarlett grumpily. "Well, that doesn't help the lemurs, does it?"

Zina twisted round. "Did you hear that squeaking noise?"

A faint squeak came again.

"It sounds like an animal." Lily stared around. "But where is it?"

Zina sprang up and tried to follow the sound. Crouching down, she delved through a pile of leaves but there was

nothing there.

"Over here!" Scarlett was leaning over the stack of sawn-off branches.

"Some poor animal's stuck under there," cried Zina.

The girls took the branches off the pile one by one, moving them gently in case the animal was right underneath. As the heap grew smaller, a little furry face looked up through the leaves. Its eyes were golden-brown.

"It's the baby lemur!" Zina pulled off the last two branches, freeing the baby lemur who they'd helped the day before.

The little animal squeaked again and bounded up Zina's arm on to her shoulder.

"Did you get stuck under there?" Zina stroked his furry head soothingly.

"Poor thing! That must have been really scary," said Lily. "Look, Zina! He

77

remembers you."

"I guess we'll have to help him find his family again," sighed Scarlett. "I just wish we'd helped them all by saving their special trees."

The girls were silent for a moment.

Zina felt tears come to her eyes again but she blinked them back. She knew what Scarlett meant. She felt like they'd failed too, but right now the baby lemur needed them. She rubbed the little creature's fur. "I guess we should start looking for the other lemurs."

"We don't need to," Lily told her. "They're coming back!"

Leaves rustled. Branches creaked. The lemur tribe came swinging silently through the trees. As they reached the clearing, they sprang down to the ground and gathered round the tree stumps. A few of them searched the ground, as if looking for food, but most of them stared at the three girls.

The baby lemur gave Zina's face a little lick. Then he scampered down her arm and leapt on to his mother's back.

The princesses exchanged looks.

"They seem really sad," murmured Lily. "Do you think they're wondering where the trees have gone?"

Zina looked round at the lemurs' faces with their tufty ears and golden-brown eyes. "I wish there was something we could do."

The wind swirled through the forest, making the branches shake and the leaves rustle. Zina's amber jewel hanging around her neck began to whisper again. The lemurs' ears pricked up.

A funny idea popped into Zina's head. Maybe the jewel whispered back to the trees for a reason. After all, her grandma had told her that the amber jewel held the heart of the forest inside it. Maybe it could help the lemurs somehow.

She pulled the necklace over her head and held the jewel up to the light. Lighter flecks winked inside the golden amber. "I know this sounds strange," she began. "But maybe my jewel can help."

"You mean ... like magic?" cried Scarlett. "That's an awesome idea! Let's go and fetch my jewel-making tools right now."

"Wait a second." Lily frowned. "Don't you think it would be better to stay here and help the lemurs find somewhere new to live? They look so quiet and sad, and we don't know if the amber jewel will do any good at all."

Scarlett's face fell. "But it's a jewel that comes from trees! I really think we should use the tools to free the magic."

Zina's mind whirled as if too many thoughts were crowding into her head at once. It was her jewel and she knew it was really up to her to decide. She let the necklace twist in the light and the teardrop-shaped jewel spun back and forth, flashing like golden fire. "I think we should see if this jewel has magic!" She jumped to her feet. "Maybe only a jewel from the forest can help the lemurs now."

Chapter Nine

The Golden Amber

Zina's feet flew as she sped down the forest path alongside her friends. A parrot called in the trees but she hardly heard it.

"We can get the jewel-making tools and run straight back," panted Scarlett. "It won't take long."

Lily stumbled over a tree root and grabbed a branch to steady herself. "I'm all right," she gasped, when the others stopped to help.

They slowed a little as they ran through the palace gates and Zina's heart sank. Her mum and dad and all the other kings and queens were climbing out of carriages by the front door. What would they say when they saw the princesses in ninja clothes?

Luckily, the grown-ups went in the front entrance so the girls dashed in through the back door. Zina stopped at the foot of the stairs. "You fetch the jewel-making tools," she told her friends. "I'll keep a lookout."

A maid came bustling past with a tea tray. Then Queen Tali marched down the corridor. "There you are, Zina." She shook her head. "I was about to ask you to come and have tea with our royal visitors but just look at you! Your hair is a mess and there are scratches all over your arms. You look as if you've been fighting a bramble patch. And where did you get those odd clothes from?"

"They're ... um ... play clothes." Zina tried to comb her tangled hair with her fingers.

Just then, Scarlett and Lily came thundering down the stairs with the box of jewel-making tools.

Queen Tali stared. "Goodness! You're all as scruffy as each other. You'd better go and get cleaned up."

"But ... there's something important we need to do," said Zina desperately. "Please can we come back and have tea later?"

"Zina, your royal duties are very important." The queen straightened her diamond crown. "You can't run off and play all the time."

"Please, Mum! The lemurs need our help right now. It's really important!"

Zina fixed her gaze on her mum's face, desperately hoping that her mum would allow her to go.

"And afterwards we promise we'll come straight back," added Scarlett. "We'll get cleaned up and brush our hair and everything!"

Queen Tali looked from one girl to the other. "All right then. But when you come back I'd like you to get changed and come for tea, please. We have lots of carnival business to talk about."

"Thank you!" Zina hugged her mum, and then the princesses raced out of the door again.

Crossing the palace garden, the princesses ran back into the rainforest. Zina led them down the path, pushing branches out of the way. A green and purple lizard dashed away from her feet and a parrot flew off, squawking in alarm.

"This is getting heavy." Scarlett paused, setting the wooden tool box on the ground.

"I'll carry it." Lily gathered it up and the girls hurried on.

Most of the lemurs were huddled in a group at one side of the clearing. Only three of them were foraging for food in the nearby bushes. The baby lemur's ears pricked up when he saw the princesses and he squeaked softly.

Zina undid her amber necklace and laid it on the mossy stone. "What shape will you change it to, Scarlett?"

"Oh!" Scarlett pulled a face. "I forgot to bring those pictures my cousin sent me showing how to shape the jewels."

"Should we go back for them?" asked Lily.

Scarlett took the box of tools and opened the lid. "Don't worry – I'll think of something."

"But we need to get the shape just right," said Zina worriedly. "If we don't then the magic might not work."

"I could make it a pretty shape like a circle or a hexagon." Scarlett picked up a tiny silver chisel.

"But isn't it about finding what suits the jewel best?" Lily frowned.

"That's what the letter from Ella said, but how can you tell what suits the jewel?" Scarlett picked up the chisel and hammer and gave them to Zina. "Maybe you should do it – it's your necklace, after all."

Zina took the little silver tools. She tried to hold them the way Scarlett always did and her hands shook a little. Taking a deep breath, she set the chisel against the edge of the amber and lifted the hammer. She knew she was supposed to tap the hammer on the end of the chisel to chip a little off the jewel.

Suddenly she wasn't sure about slicing into the jewel. Her grandma had given the necklace to her and she didn't want to ruin it. If only there was a way to free the magic without cutting the amber. Leaves rustled overhead and the amber jewel began to whisper.

As the jewel whispered and sparkled, Zina saw something she'd never noticed before. Leaning closer, she ran a finger along the edge of the amber. There was a tiny bump on the bottom of the teardrop that spoiled the smooth shape. Straightaway she set the chisel against the bump and gave one small tap with the hammer.

The tiny bump broke off. Zina ran her finger along the jewel again. Now the amber was a perfect teardrop shape but it didn't look any different than before. She waited for a moment but nothing happened.

"Did it work?" said Lily breathlessly.

"No, I don't think so." Zina held up the jewel to show her friends. "I made its shape smoother but nothing's changed. Maybe I should try something different. Or maybe the jewel just isn't magic." She peered closely at the amber.

"Let me see." Scarlett held out her hand but as Zina passed the jewel, it slipped out of her fingers.

The amber lay winking in the sunlight on the dark-brown earth. A great shaking and rustling grew in the treetops and the jewel murmured louder than ever. Then suddenly a plant growing next to the jewel sprouted wildly and a cluster of buds broke out on each stem. The buds grew larger, before bursting open to reveal beautiful yellow flowers.

"What was THAT?" gasped Lily.

Zina gazed at the jewel and a wide smile spread over her face. "I think there IS magic inside this jewel after all!"

Chapter Ten

Magical Plant Power

The princesses gathered round the sprouting plant. "Look how much it's grown!" cried Scarlett. "That jewel must have *loads* of magic."

"Try another plant, Zina," said Lily excitedly.

Zina picked up the amber and looked around. Finding a tiny seedling on the ground, she placed the jewel beside it.

For a moment, nothing happened. Then the seedling grew, its stalk thickening.

More stems burst out of the sides and leaves grew all over them. By the time it stopped, it was a bush nearly as tall as the princesses, with thick, woody branches.

Zina tingled with excitement as she pushed aside the prickly stems to find the jewel. Scrambling up, she held the amber in the palm of her hand. "I think I know what to do. We need to find saplings – baby trees – and they have to be tamarind trees just like the ones the carnival workers cut down."

The princesses dashed off in different directions, looking for saplings.

"I've found one!" called Scarlett almost at once.

Zina ran over to look. "That's a different kind of tree. The leaves should be rounder and the trunk darker."

"Oh!" Scarlett frowned. "How about

this one?" She pounced on the next sapling, which stretched up to her knee.

Zina shook her head. "Keep looking. I'm sure we'll find some."

The girls raced this way and that, calling to each other through the trees. At last they found two tamarind saplings. They dug them up as best they could, using the little silver chisels in the tool box. Carrying them carefully back to the clearing, they set them down on the earth.

"Now we can make them grow!" Scarlett shook back her curls.

"We should probably plant them first," said Zina.

"I'll get a garden spade," said Lily. "I saw one in the courtyard when we were decorating the float."

While Lily ran to fetch the spade, Zina and Scarlett searched for more saplings.

They found eight altogether, although one had a split, which made its main branch droop quite badly.

The lemurs watched quietly while the girls set out the saplings around the clearing. Lily came back with the spade and they dug a hole for each baby tamarind tree and planted them carefully, pushing the soil around the tree roots. At last they stood back and looked at the ring of tiny trees they had made.

"Time for plant power!" said Scarlett, wiping earth off her nose.

"Go on, Zina!" Lily smiled widely. "I think this is going to be amazing."

Zina felt her heart fluttering as she took the amber jewel and laid it on the earth beside the first sapling. The little tree sprang upwards, its stem thickening. More and more branches sprouted from the main trunk, and masses of leaves unfurled along each one. The ground below them trembled a little.

"That must be the roots growing in the earth," whispered Lily in wonder.

The tree went on growing until it towered over them. Its leaves whispered in the wind and the amber jewel murmured back.

"That was AWESOME!" cried Scarlett.

Zina beamed. "Look at the lemurs."

The tribe of lemurs had pricked up their ears. Their eyes brightened.

"Do the next tree, Zina!" said Scarlett, bouncing on the spot.

Zina placed the amber jewel beside one sapling after another. She took her time with each one, making sure the little trees had finished sprouting before she moved on. At last she came to the tree with the drooping branch. She bit her lip. She didn't want the tree to grow with a huge

♥♥
♥ 97 ♥
♥

split in the middle.

She pressed the amber against the split and held the drooping branch up straight. Slowly, the tear mended and the branch was whole again. Then she placed the amber on the ground and let the last sapling grow. Together the trees swayed in the breeze, their branches like arms reaching up to touch the sky.

The lemurs bounded forward, chattering excitedly. They scampered up the tree trunks and swung from the branches. They jumped from one tree to the next, as if they were playing lemur tag.

"We did it!" Zina gazed round at the beautiful ring of tamarind trees. "We gave the lemurs back their home."

"Not just the lemurs – look." Lily pointed to a bright-green gecko running up a tree trunk and a blue coua fluttering down to settle on a branch.

Just then the mother lemur bounded over carrying her baby. She stopped in front of the princesses and the baby darted off her back. Zina crouched down and the little animal sprang up her arm on to her shoulder. Curling his tail around Zina's neck, the baby lemur licked her cheek before scampering away again.

"I think he was saying thank you!" said Scarlett, smiling.

"I wish we had lemurs in my kingdom," said Lily.

Zina smiled and touched her cheek where the baby lemur's soft fur had brushed against her skin. Then she fastened the amber necklace around her neck. The golden jewel shone in the speckled light drifting through the freshly grown leaves. "My grandma was right.

This jewel really does hold the heart of the forest."

Chapter Eleven

Carnival Day

The next morning Zina jumped out of bed and drew the curtains to let the bright sunshine pour into her room. Today was the day of the carnival and there was so much to do!

Rushing out into the corridor, she knocked on her friends' bedroom doors. "Wake up! It's carnival day."

Lily opened her door, her eyes half open. "Hmm what did you say? I was just having a very strange dream about trees..."

"It was probably all true!" laughed
Zina.

"I've been awake for ages!" said
Scarlett, flinging open her door. "I've
been down to the kitchen and Cook made
me boiled eggs and toast because I was so
hungry."

The princesses rushed downstairs and
chopped up some fruit for the lemurs'
breakfast. They left the pieces of mango,
banana and orange on the palace wall
before hurrying inside for their own
breakfast, where Scarlett managed to
have second helpings!

Then they added some finishing touches
to their lemur float by painting lizards
and parrots on to the background. They
also made sure the furry toy lemurs were
fastened safely on to the model trees.

Zina's mum and dad came out to look

at the finished float. Queen Tali was dressed ready for the carnival in a yellow silk dress tied with a sash and a golden crown. "Oh, Zina! That looks wonderful," she cried. "You really have done a fabulous job. Look at those lizards on the background – they look so real!"

Lily smiled and her cheeks went pink because she'd painted the lizards.

"Very impressive, girls!" King Tomas nodded, his silver crown gleaming in the sunlight. "And I hear you've helped with other parts of the carnival planning too."

"Really? I didn't know about that." Queen Tali looked confused.

"Yes, Mr Hazzam told me about some changes to the parade route," the king continued, and Zina shuffled her feet worriedly. "He told me the girls helped change the route to a much better one."

Zina saw he was smiling. "It was all

for the lemurs. They really need the tamarind trees so we had to try to protect them."

"Then it's good that the lemurs have you to look out for them." Queen Tali looked at her watch. "Time to get ready, girls. Make sure you wash that paint off your fingers and don't forget to brush your hair."

💜

Zina climbed on to the lemur float wearing her white dress with embroidery round the hem. The diamonds dotted over her silver tiara sparkled in the sunlight. Scarlett jumped up next, her red dress swirling around her legs. Her dark curls were tied back and an emerald crown rested on her head.

Lily climbed up last, smoothing down her light-blue dress. She pushed her long blonde hair over her shoulder and

checked that her pearl tiara hadn't
slipped over her ears. The girls seated
themselves on a box covered with brown
and green velvet that had been decorated
to look like a fallen tree.

"Your float is magnificent!" cried Mr
Hazzam, who had come to lead them to
the parade. "You will be the stars of the
carnival." He took the horses' reins and
led them through the tall palace gates
and along the road.

Soon they joined the other floats, full
of people in bright costumes. Musicians
played their drums and pipes and
everyone in the crowd was dancing and
waving. The princesses waved back,
smiling at everyone.

"What brilliant costumes!" Scarlett
pointed to a group of dancers dressed
as fruit. "Look at that lady with the
pineapple headdress!"

The next group of dancers were dressed as wild animals – lions, giraffes, zebras and more – and their face paint was amazing. Zina gazed admiringly at the smiling golden face of the lion dancer with his yellow mane and fierce whiskers.

An ocean float rolled past next, painted with shells and brightly coloured fish. On a pretend rock sat ladies dressed as mermaids with tails made from shiny cloth, and starfish necklaces.

At lunchtime the girls climbed down and Mr Hazzam took them along to the food stalls. They ate wraps filled with peppers and spicy chicken, followed by mango ice cream.

"Mmm!" Zina took another spoonful of ice cream. "I think this is the best ice cream I've ever had."

After lunch they joined the parade again, rolling along the route through the forest. People by the side of the path waved and cheered. The trees swayed on either side and suddenly a red and blue parrot flew down to settle on one of their cardboard trees.

"Look, Lily!" Zina pointed to the bird. "Your painting looks so real that the animals think our float is part of the forest."

There was a chattering in the trees and the baby lemur swung down from a branch, landing neatly on the float. He tried nibbling a tissue-paper leaf and then pulled a funny face. The girls laughed. The little lemur sprang on to Zina's shoulder before leaping back into the trees.

"This has been amazing!" sighed Lily. "You will let us come back to the carnival next year, won't you, Zina?"

"Definitely!" Zina smiled. "It's much

more fun going to the carnival with friends."

When the parade was over, the princesses ran out into the rainforest to check on the new trees. They found most of the lemurs playing among the branches. Some were sleeping, their stripy tails curled around their bodies.

Zina touched the trunk of one of the new trees, amazed at how strong and sturdy it felt. "It looks as if these trees have been here for years. No one would ever believe they were saplings yesterday."

"And the lemurs are so happy," added Scarlett.

"And there's plenty of fruit for them to eat," said Lily, clutching her hair as one of the fruit dropped close to her head.

Zina smiled and linked arms with her friends. "No one will ever know how the

lemurs' home was saved except us! I'll always be so proud that we're the Rescue Princesses."

Look out for another
daring animal adventure!

The Rescue
Princesses
The Moonlit Mystery

Chapter One

Tree Acrobatics

Princess Lulu grasped the lowest branch of the tree with both hands and swung herself backwards and forwards. After a few swings, she stretched high enough to curl her legs right round the branch above.

Her wavy black hair swayed as she climbed. She wore a short yellow dress dotted with tiny golden beads. It was her tree-climbing dress and it was now extremely dusty. On her left hand she wore a ring with a gleaming yellow topaz, her favourite jewel.

Halfway up the tree, there was a long straight branch, almost as straight and smooth as the beam in her gym. She loved practising in the gym, but being out here with the sun blazing down and the breeze on her face was even better.

On her left stood the palace of Undala with its courtyard and fountain, and on her right was the outer wall, with the golden grasslands beyond. In the distance, an elephant lifted its trunk at the waterhole, getting its early morning drink.

Lulu smiled and turned back to the branch in front of her. She wanted to see if she could do a cartwheel along it. She stood tall and gazed straight ahead, excitement fizzing inside her. Then, pointing one foot, she raised an arm high

above her head, ready to cartwheel.

"Atchoo!" The ear-splitting sneeze came from below, making Lulu jump. She wobbled and nearly fell off the branch. Grabbing hold of the tree trunk, she peered down at the ground.

Prince Olaf stood under the tree, his spiky blond head looking up at her. Lulu sighed. Olaf was visiting the Kingdom of Undala with his parents, the King and Queen of Finia, and ever since arriving he'd been following her around. He'd seemed so nice when she'd met him before at royal balls and banquets. But now she thought he was a know-it-all!

Olaf sneezed again. "Sorry!" he said. "I was just watching. I love learning acrobatics and circus skills. I was practising them in your gym yesterday. Maybe I can teach some to you?"

Lulu swung down from the branch and

landed on the ground in front of him, hands on her hips. "You were practising in *my* gym?"

"That's right." Olaf grinned, not noticing Lulu's frown. "And I think I'm getting really good at walking the beam."

"Really?" Lulu folded her arms. "How many times did you fall off, then?"

"Oh, a few times." Olaf didn't look even the tiniest bit embarrassed. "Would you like me to show you how to do it? I can always hold your hand if you're nervous."

Lulu's eyes flashed. Olaf was the most annoying, puffed-up prince she'd ever met! "No thanks!" she snapped. "I can turn hundreds of cartwheels on my beam and I certainly don't need anyone to hold my hand!" She was about to add that she would show him just how good she was, but the low clang of the breakfast gong interrupted her.

Lulu rushed inside with Olaf trailing behind her. She was going out to the grasslands with Walter the ranger this morning and she didn't want to be late. She bounded into the palace hallway, with its shelves of beautiful animal carvings. A huge painting of a lion standing at the foot of a mountain hung next to the doorway. Inside the Great Hall, the maids were setting out the breakfast plates. Lulu hurried in and found a seat at the long wooden table.

"Good morning, Lulu. Good morning, Olaf," said Lulu's mum, Queen Shani, with a warm smile. "Have either of you seen Lady Malika?"

Lulu shook her head and helped herself to the warm buttered rolls.

"No, I haven't, Your Majesty," replied Prince Olaf, with a sweeping bow. "But I'll go and look for her if you like."

Lady Malika was the queen's sister who lived on the other side of Undala. It was a long way away, so she didn't visit them very often. She owned a big circus in the city, which Lulu had visited once when she was little. Like the Finians, Lady Malika had come to stay at the palace for a few weeks.

"Thank you, Prince Olaf. But there's no need. I just wondered where she was as I noticed that her room was empty," said Queen Shani. "Perhaps she had something important to do this morning, so she left the palace early."

Lulu scowled at Prince Olaf, who was offering the bread rolls to her mother politely, and wished more than anything that her friends, Princesses Emily, Clarabel and Jaminta, had come to stay instead. She knew they'd love Undala, with its huge grasslands filled with wild animals. She sighed wistfully, just as a horn tooted loudly outside the window.

"That's Walter! He must be ready to leave," she cried, racing out of the hall and down the front steps.

"Slow down, Lulu! Must you rush everywhere?" the queen called after her.

Lulu jumped into the truck next to Walter, who smiled at her. "Let's go!" she cried.

They zoomed away between the tall palace gates, with the red earth flying beneath their wheels.